The Ghost Box

by

Catherine Fisher

With special thanks to our readers:

Tish Farrell
Mandy Haines
Heather Lowe
Sarika Parmar

Visit Catherine's website:
www.catherine-fisher.com

First published in 2008 in Great Britain by
Barrington Stoke Ltd
18 Walker Street, Edinburgh, EH3 7LP

www.barringtonstoke.co.uk

This edition first published 2011

ISBN: 978-1-84299-987-5

Printed in China by Leo

Contents

1   The Face in the Tree   1

2   The Silver Box   6

3   A Shadow   12

4   Broken Nails   18

5   The Shop by the Stream   24

6   A Terrible Secret   31

7   You've Made Me Angry   37

8   Alone   43

9   A Soul for a Soul   49

10 Together   55

Chapter 1

The Face in the Tree

Sarah was carrying a tray of wine-glasses in one hand and a Coke in the other hand when she saw the painting.

It was on the wall of the gallery. Between the chatting groups of people, the surprise of seeing the painting stopped her dead. She stared at the green fields, the hillside – they were the same as she could see from her house.

"Hey, waitress. Is that for me?" Matt took the Coke out of her hand and slurped it.

Sarah glared at him. "No. It wasn't."

"Tough. You'll have to get another one." He grinned, his black Goth hair falling into his black-lined Goth eyes. She thought he looked stupid.

"Move, Matt. I'm working."

"Got to make sure Mummy's little party goes well, have you?" he said. He didn't move, so she pushed past him and started handing round the drinks to the guests.

Sarah's mum was a sculptor, and the party was for her new exhibition. Her friends were mostly other artists and painters and gallery owners. They all wore bright clothes and talked loudly. Sarah saw her mum now, having a photograph taken in front of the big bronze sculpture called *Man in the Rain*. Mum looked flushed and excited. She winked at Sarah.

Then the photographer said, "Look this way, please."

Sarah dumped the tray behind a sofa as soon as it was empty. She was fed up with helping. From now on she'd swan around being the sculptor's daughter. Keeping away from Matt.

And his dad, Gareth.

Gareth was getting into all the photographs too. He and Mum had their arms round each other, and Mum was grinning like a kid.

From behind a bronze figure, Sarah watched them. She liked Gareth. He was a bit up-tight, a bit like a teacher in his old brown suit, but now he and Mum were married she'd soon sort him out. Gareth was OK, but Matt was his son, and having Matt in the house was a pain. He was untidy and rude. He always left his music blaring really loud and left his stupid black clothes lying around everywhere.

Annoyed just by thinking of him, she went back to look at the painting.

No one was near it. It was old, and it hung in the dim part of the gallery where the rain trickled down the windows outside. Sarah stood in front of it, seeing the fine brush-strokes, the dust on the gold frame.

It was a painting of the barn before it had been turned into a house.

Her house.

Now there was a modern part built on and huge glass windows, but in the painting the barn was old, the thatch falling off its roof. The big doors stood open, and a dog was running under the wheels of a hay cart standing where Mum parked her car. It was strange to see their house like this, as it must have looked a hundred years ago. The round window in the stone wall was the same, but everything else had changed.

And there was a tree.

Sarah stepped nearer, to take a closer look. There was a huge oak tree in the painting. It stood near the end of the barn, right where her bedroom was now.

She had no idea a tree had once grown there. There was none now. It looked very old, its trunk enormous, its branches reaching out like green powdery fingers.

She came so close to the glass that her breath misted it. She wiped the damp away and saw that the tree in the painting was full of birds – small, strange birds she'd never seen before. Their bright eyes peeped from the leaves. They were blue and gold birds with long tails and flashes of scarlet on their wings.

And then she saw a face.

It was among the leaves. Or perhaps made out of leaves. A narrow, dirty face, its eyes glints of sun-light, its smile a slant of shadow. As if someone was hiding in the green canopy, someone holding something bright in a thin hand.

She looked at him, sure he was there.

"Who are you?" she said under her breath.

For a moment she almost thought he would answer. But he didn't.

He winked at her.

Sarah jumped back. Her heart thumped.

A shadow fell across the painting, and Gareth came up behind her. "So here you are!"

He put his glasses on and stared at the old barn with interest. "Oh, look! Our house. Quite good, isn't it?"

Sarah couldn't answer. She stared at the tree but there was nothing in its leaves now, no birds, no face, no sly eye that closed.

Only the reflection of the room behind her, with its tinkle of glasses, its glitter and chat.

Chapter 2
The Silver Box

It was late when the four of them drove home. Curled in the back of the car, Sarah tried to ignore the tinny music from Matt's ear-phones. In the front seat Mum was half asleep. Gareth was driving.

The car was quiet and smelt of leather. Bottles of left-over wine clinked in the boot.

Sarah gazed out at the dark fields. A purple glimmer still hung in the sky, and the woods were tangled shadows along the lane, flashing into sudden gold when the head-lights brushed them.

Gareth said, "I thought it all went very well."

Mum nodded, sleepy. "Thanks for all the help. You were great, Sarah."

"Now you can take a well-earned rest." He grinned at her, as the car bumped over the gravel and slurred to a stop outside the house. But Mum was staring up at the windows in surprise. "Who left all the lights on?" she said.

Stepping out, Sarah saw that the house blazed with light. The huge glass windows sent slanting oblongs over the smooth lawns.

Gareth turned to Matt. "You were last out."

"I switched them off," Matt said with a shrug. "I know I did."

"You don't think there's been a break-in, do you?" Mum's voice was quiet.

"The door's not broken. But stay here. I'll check."

Gareth let himself in and after a second Matt went after him. Sarah leaned on the car, a little bit scared, but after a while Gareth's head came out of the upstairs window. "No one here. Just Matt being forgetful, I suppose."

Mum smiled.

But as Sarah followed her in, a tiny sound came from behind. She turned quickly, looking up. For a moment she was sure she had heard the rustle of leaves. Just there, by her window.

When she went to bed she remembered, and stood for a moment looking out. It was raining again now, and the countryside was black, hidden by slashes of rain on the glass. All she could see was herself.

Jumping into bed, she flicked the lamp off. All at once, she lay in a black space. Her room was quiet, at the end of the corridor, in the part of the house built onto the barn.

Her bed was right next to the window. She liked it there. She could lie back and stare up into the sky, seeing the stars. Sometimes she could hear an owl hunting in Holtom Wood, or a fox barking. Once she had sat up and seen a badger in the moonlight, crossing the lawn. But tonight there was only the rattle of rain running down the glass, its soft tap-tap on the roof.

She turned over. The bedroom was still, the wardrobe a black mass with her school coat hanging from it, arms out. The wind chime turned without a sound. A faint smell of perfume drifted from her cluttered dressing table.

She closed her eyes.

She must be asleep, she thought, because she was dreaming about a creaking in the room. It was soft at first, and then it grew, a harsh, struggling sound, as if something was trapped, trying to get out.

She didn't move, gripping the pillow.

The sound grew. It ripped open the darkness. It burst into the room.

Sarah snapped her eyes open wide. She saw that a split was tearing in the carpet next to her bed. Something began to slither through. As she sat up with a gasp of fear, she saw that it was a tiny green shoot, with two leaves. It pushed its way up, growing fast. Branches burst out from it. Buds exploded into golden leaves.

The tree grew quickly, rustling upwards. Young leaves opened all round her, cool on her lips and face. As she stared in wonder, the room filled with a damp, earthy smell of soil and worms. The tree soared high into the roof. A branch punched through a window. Tiny tinkles of glass fell in splinters.

How could this be a dream?

She could feel the cold rain, taste pollen. As she put her hands out she caught leaves, falling all round her, on the bed, on her pillow, on the bedside lamp.

With one last mighty effort the tree smashed through the roof, and now the birds rushed out of it, blue and gold birds, flying round her, soaring into the sky.

Sarah stared up.

In the top of the trunk, wedged between two branches, she saw something small and bright.

She stood quickly, gripping the wet trunk to keep her footing on the bed.

Yes. There it was. Just as it had been in the picture, though now no one held it.

"Hello?" she said quietly. "Are you up there?"

No answer.

She put her foot on a bent branch, pulled herself up, and began to climb. After all, it was safe. You couldn't fall and hurt yourself in a dream. And if she did she would only land on the bed.

It wasn't easy. Soon she was out of breath and her arms were hurting. Twice she slipped, scratching the palms of her hands. Leaves fell on her face, and she had to blink pollen out of her eyes. But still she dragged herself upwards until her reaching hand could slither round the branch and touch the box.

It was icy cold. Her fingers slid along the damp metal, feeling a key-hole. She could only just reach it. She tipped it out and it fell down. She grabbed it, quickly, gasping for breath, her hair in her eyes.

Then, very softly, someone tapped her on the back.

Chapter 3
A Shadow

Sarah screamed and sat up in bed.

Matt jumped back. "Whoa! What's wrong with you?"

For a moment she had no idea where she was. Then she saw her bedroom, quiet and normal, the windows full of morning sun-light.

"What are you doing in my room?" she snapped.

Matt gave a shrug. "Waking you up. Your mum called, but you were dead to the world. It's nearly nine o'clock."

He wore black jeans and a black top. He was always in black, she thought, a creeping shadow in the bright house. Now he said, "I won't bother next time."

"No. Don't. Get lost."

Half-way to the door he said, "Where did that come from?"

She looked where he was looking.

The silver box stood on the bedside table, next to the lamp. It looked heavy and expensive. She stared at it, astonished, and the dream of the tree came back to her in all its brilliant colour.

Matt reached out his hand to it but she snapped, "Don't touch it! It's mine!"

The cry was so sharp she even shocked herself. Matt stood very still. She could sense his anger. His eyes were dark and bitter.

Suddenly he said, "Look, Sarah, I didn't want our parents to get together either. Dad and I had a good place of our own – we didn't need to come to this posh dump. But don't worry. I won't be sticking around to mess up your pretty life. Next year, when I go to college, you won't see me for dust."

13

He slammed the door as he went out and her dressing gown fell off the hook on the back.

Sarah stared at it, lying in a heap on the floor. Just for a moment she felt bad about being spiteful to him. Then she swung her legs out of bed and took the box on her lap.

It was real. Silver, by the look of it, and very old, its lid made of silver leaves over-lapping each other. Oak leaves. Around its rim were words in a strange language. She couldn't read them.

She ran her fingers over them, feeling the cold metal. How could she have brought the box out of a dream? Or had Mum put it here last night, perhaps from the gallery, and forgotten about it, and Sarah had dreamed of it? It didn't seem possible.

There was a key-hole but no key. She tried to open the lid but the box was firmly locked. Feeling let down, she shook it.

Something rolled and rattled inside.

She held it still, afraid what was inside it might break. From downstairs her mother called, "Sarah! Breakfast!"

There was no school because it was half term. Gareth had gone to work and she didn't know about Matt. In the kitchen the dogs, Jack and Jess, lay sprawled on the mat by the door, looking in hope at their empty food bowls. They sat up as Sarah came in but she shook her head at them. "You've already been fed."

"Let them out, will you?" her mum said.

As she opened the door a gust of wind blew wet leaves against her feet. Drops of rain spattered from the gutter. "It's autumn," she said, surprised, because the storm of the night had stripped the trees, and a new carpet of leaves clotted the lawn.

Mum smiled, and turned as the phone rang.

"Go on," Sarah said to the dogs.

Jack growled. The sound came from deep inside him. He bared his teeth, and Jess barked, two sharp, worried barks. They were looking at the corner of the barn towards her bedroom, but there was nothing there apart from the leaves, whipping up in the wind.

"Oh, go on!" Sarah pushed them out.

Then, after a moment, she walked down the path and stared at the glassy corner of the building. The windows here were floor-to-ceiling. Through them she could see Mum on the phone, talking and laughing. She could see her own reflection too, looking cold and puzzled.

And there was a shadow.

It lay on the grass behind her, and it wasn't hers.

It was small, and close, and for a moment she felt a chill at her back, and turned quickly.

The lawn was empty.

Inside, Mum said, "I have to pop out to Marston. Will you be all right?"

"Fine. No problem."

"I don't know where Matt's got to."

Sarah plugged her ear-phones in. "Who cares!"

She read and then went on-line, and then phoned her friend Olly and ate some cheese and apples and crisps, but by the afternoon she was bored and fed up with being on her own. At two Mum rang.

"I'll be another hour. Has Matt come back?"

Sarah gave a shrug. "No."

"Well, you're not scared there, all on your own, are you?"

"Of course not."

Putting the phone down, she wished her mother hadn't said that. She hadn't been scared, but now the house seemed dim and gloomy, with the rain pattering on the windows and the early October gloom closing in. She went around putting all the lights on. Then she stopped.

A door had closed upstairs.

Standing still, she listened, her heart thudding.

A floor-board creaked.

Then she was sure.

Someone was walking across the floor of her room.

Chapter 4
Broken Nails

"Matt?" she said.

The foot-steps stopped.

The silence was worse than anything. "Matt? Are you up there?"

The silence waited for her. The silence listened to her fear.

Slowly, she began to climb the stairs. They were old, and they went up in a long curve. She could see rain on the sky-light in the roof. It made strange rippling shadows down the walls.

Her foot crunched on something and she leaned down and picked it up. Its wetness was a shock. A dead leaf. She turned and looked down at the front door, but it was closed firmly. Had Matt come in? She hadn't heard him.

She dropped the leaf and climbed another three steps. As she came closer to the landing her heart-beat seemed louder. She was sweating and her hand on the rail was cold.

All the bedroom doors were closed, apart from hers.

Her door was ajar.

She could see the corner of her bed, the side of her wardrobe.

He was in there. It had to be Matt. He had to be looking for the silver box.

She crept closer. There were wind chimes hanging from her ceiling, small metal chimes of elephants and tigers. She could see them spinning, hear the faint silvery tinkle they made in the breeze.

She grabbed the door handle and took a deep breath. Then she flung the door open and stormed in.

No one was there.

The curtains moved in the stillness. The belt of her dressing gown swung softly to and fro.

She let out her breath.

There was a smell.

A wet, cloying smell, like something rotten.

And the bottom drawer of her wardrobe had been opened, because a trail of purple shirt hung out of it, the old purple shirt she didn't wear any more, that she had used to wrap the silver box in.

With a gasp of anger she knelt and tugged at it. If he'd …

But the box was still there, still locked.

Still rattling when she shook it.

****

Later, after tea, Matt was lying on the settee watching TV. She walked in and stood in front of the screen.

He twisted his neck to look round at her. "What's up now?"

"Don't you ever try that again. Or I'll speak to Gareth."

"Try what, drama queen?" Matt said.

"That box is mine. Stay out of my things, creep."

One black-lined eye flickered at her. "Haven't a clue what you're talking about."

"Yeah. Right."

In the kitchen she said to Gareth, "Where do you get keys made?"

"You need a key?"

"Oh, not for a door or anything big. Just … I've got an old jewellery box and I'd like to be able to lock it. My dad gave it to me."

She knew he wouldn't ask any more questions about it if she said that, and he didn't. "Oh, right. Well, a cobbler, I suppose, or a jewellers if it's really old. There's a shop in Marston, down that little side street by the stream. I could take it for you, if you – "

"No." She shook her head. "That's OK. I'll take it myself."

****

She woke late in the night.

She was lying on her side, with her face to the wall. All she could see were the blurred, close-up trainers of a band on a poster that she was already bored with. But her eyes were wide, her back prickling with sweat.

Someone was sitting on her bed.

It wasn't a dream.

She could feel a weight dipping the mattress, smell that odd, leafy smell.

She kept very still, listening to the rattle of the box in his hands, feeling terror ice her skin. Then she sat up and turned her head.

A boy was sitting next to her.

He was small and had dirty, tangled dark hair and a thin, frail face. He had one ear-ring, and when he looked up his eyes were lit with a faint green glimmer. For a moment he just looked at her, and then he turned back to the box.

She stared at his hands.

He was tugging at the box, trying to force it open with his broken nails, smearing it with dirt. He worked at it, getting more and more desperate. Then he said, "I can't do it. I just can't."

There was a sadness in his voice that chilled her. She sat up, slowly.

"Who are you?"

He shot her a glance. "I need the key. Have you got the key?"

She shook her head. He wasn't real. He couldn't be real, because his was the face she had seen in the painting, and in her dream.

"I gave the box to you," he said. "Because I knew you could bring it out."

"Out?"

"Of the tree."

She drew her knees up under her. "How did you get in here?"

He threw the box on the bed in despair and looked at her. Then he lifted his hand and pushed it through her, through the poster, through the wall.

"It was easy," he said in a whisper.

Chapter 5

The Shop by the Stream

Sarah almost screamed.

But the boy just gave a shrug. He tapped the box with one dirty finger. "I need the key. I need you to get me the key."

She huddled herself up, pulling the bed-clothes tight around her. She wanted to shiver and shiver, to back away from those fingers that had moved right into her skin. She said in a hushed voice, "Where is it?"

"Lost." He looked at her. "Some trees grow keys. Ash does. But not oak."

It meant nothing to her. Perhaps the boy sensed that, because he shrank back and leaned against the wall, his head dropped as if in misery. Locking his long, dirty fingers together, he said, "I'm trapped here."

"Trapped?"

He turned his eyes sideways. They were dark and bitter. "I was a thief once. I picked pockets, stole purses, snatched watches. Do people still do that?"

"Mobile phones," she said, thinking of Matt's anger when his had been stolen.

The boy's gaze flickered. "This is what happened to me. I robbed a man in the street of a package. I pushed him and he fell, and I ran away with it. I felt gleeful, and proud. But he called after me, strange words in a foreign language, and I looked back and saw he was pointing at me, a long, bony finger. He was calling down a curse on me."

He rubbed his hands together. She saw how the thin wrists stuck out from the ragged sleeves, how his shoes were a web of holes.

"He killed me," he said in a whisper.

Sarah's lips were dry, so she licked them and murmured, "How?"

"Sickness. The town was always full of sickness. I opened the package but it only contained a box. This box. And it was empty. Weakness came over me. I hadn't eaten for days. I felt feverish and hot. So I slipped away, out here into the hills. It was a freezing night and I knew I wouldn't see the end of it. I lay down in the leaves at the foot of the tree, made a hollow in them, curled up shivering. And I died, holding the box."

Sarah didn't want to think about that. So she said, "But the box isn't empty."

"Not now." He turned his dark gaze on her. "Don't you see? He cursed me for all time. He has locked my soul inside the box."

She stared at him. Outside, the wind was rising. She heard it thrash in the bare branches, heard it whip along the corner of the house.

"I know your name," he said, suddenly sly. "Your name is Sarah. I've heard them call you, your mother, your brother ..."

"He's not my brother."

"Find it for me, Sarah. Find me the key! Help me. I've been here for so long ... and I'm so cold."

His misery was making her shiver – that and the cold that seeped from him, the flakes of dried mud on the bed.

"What's *your* name?" she asked.

He turned to her and smiled, and shook his head. "I've forgotten," he said.

****

The shop had a sign outside saying *Morgan Rees – Fine Antiques*. Sarah stopped at the door, the silver box in a plastic bag under her arm.

She was nervous about going in, and she was tired. After the boy had vanished she had jumped up and turned on every light and lamp in the room. She had left them on all night, lying wide-eyed, her mind racing in terror through every ghost story and film she knew. Only when she'd heard Gareth getting up for work had she fallen asleep again.

Now she took a deep breath and looked up and down the alley with its pretty stream where two swans glided along. She would get him the key. And then he would go.

The shop was old. Chairs and cabinets were set out in the window. It looked expensive, but she turned the handle and went in, down one step.

A bell jangled somewhere far off in the building. Sarah stood in a slant of dusty sunlight and gazed round.

A great doll's house stood on a table, all the tiny furniture taken out for cleaning. Behind it a gold bird-cage hung, with a small stuffed bird that stared over her head. There were paintings on the walls. A shelf of musty leather-bound books stood opposite a small fireplace glowing red from the heat of the coals.

A man came up to her. "Can I help you?"

He wore a black coat and his hair was white. He had a pair of glasses on his sharp nose. He was tall, and very thin.

"I don't know. I need a key for an old jewellery box."

"Keys!" He smiled a lop-sided smile. "Well, I have plenty of those."

He took out a tray lined with red velvet and she saw it held hundreds of keys. Big, small, gold, tin. Keys with bits of ribbon tied on, keys with labels, huge church keys, tiny luggage keys.

"May I see the box?" he said.

Sarah undid it in a rustle of plastic. "It's this."

She held it out.

"Ah," the man said. Carefully he took it, his fingers round it. He carried it to a side table and focused a small lamp on it. The silver oak leaves gleamed.

"Fine. Very fine. 18th-century, perhaps earlier. French. Made in Paris."

"Is it worth a lot?" She hadn't meant to ask but she was interested now.

He looked at her through the glasses. "Do you want to sell?"

"No ... at least ... it's not really mine."

She hoped he wouldn't think she'd stolen it, but he wasn't really listening. He was looking through a magnifying glass he'd taken from a drawer, looking at the writing on the box, the words in the strange language. As he did so, she felt him stiffen.

"I just need a key," she murmured.

Morgan Rees put the glass down with a click on the table and stepped back. He took his hands away from the box.

"I'm afraid I don't have one to fit," he said in a quiet voice.

Chapter 6
A Terrible Secret

For a moment, Sarah didn't understand. She stared at the shop-keeper, puzzled. "But ... you haven't tried any of them yet!"

"Nor will I." Morgan Rees's eyes were sharp and thoughtful. Then he took the glasses off and pulled out a white handkerchief. He polished the lenses. "Where did you get this box?"

At once she held back. "It ... it was a present."

He looked up. "A locked box?"

She blushed, angry. "Do you think I stole it?"

"It would be better if you had. Then you could just put it back."

His voice was grave and worried. He said, "Let me tell you something. This is a box that should never be opened. I believe it contains a great danger. The letters around its rim are very old, and tell of a terrible secret. I have heard of such things before. I will not open it for you, and my advice is that you leave it locked and never try again."

The fire crackled. Outside, footsteps pattered past the shop window.

Morgan Rees put one long finger on the box. "Let me give you some money for it. Then I will lock it away in my safe and it will be no danger to you, or anyone. Let me do that."

His soft voice made her pause. And then she thought of the boy, his cold, bony hands twisting at the lid, his bitter voice saying, "He locked my soul inside the box." How could she leave him to be trapped for all time?

"I'm sorry." Sarah reached out and took the box, shoving it back into the plastic bag. "If you won't help me, I'll find someone else who will."

Morgan Rees shook his head. He seemed dismayed. He said, "Then just let me ..."

"Thank you. Goodbye."

Sarah was angry. Her fingers shook as she grasped the door and tugged it open. A cold breeze swept into the shop, making the fire roar and fluttering pages of books. Without looking back to see if he followed, she ran up the step and hurried down the little lane. When someone called her name she marched on, not knowing why she was so shaken.

Had he been trying to scare her? She wasn't scared. She knew what was in the box, and he didn't. He'd wanted the box for his shop. He'd thought all that rubbish about danger would scare her into selling it cheap. Well, she wasn't such a fool.

"Sarah!"

She stopped. The man in the shop hadn't known her name. She turned.

Matt was pushing his bike up the lane. He came past the shop and she saw that Morgan Rees was standing in the doorway, a tall shadow, watching them both. Annoyed, she walked on.

"Wait for me!" Matt caught up, out of breath.

"What do you want?"

"Look." He took her arm and made her stop. "Can't we call some sort of truce, agree to be friends? It wasn't me who went into your room. And I'm not interested in any old box."

But as he said it he was staring at the plastic bag, and she knew he could see through it at what was inside. "Where did you get that thing anyway?" he asked.

"Mind your own business. And ... well, all right, I know it wasn't you now. It was him."

"Him?" He stared. "Gareth?"

"Not Gareth, stupid."

"Then who else? Is someone else getting into the house?"

"No." She turned to him, in alarm. "What makes you think that?"

Matt gave a shrug. "I thought ... last night I thought I heard voices. Strange, low voices. I got up and looked downstairs but there was nothing. Except ..."

"Except what?"

He looked down at the bike. "You'll think this is stupid. But I thought I could hear the wind in the branches of a tree. A big tree. And it was inside our house."

Sarah stared at him. And just for a moment, standing in that narrow lane with the swans rippling by on the sunny stream, she wanted to tell him about the box and the boy and the tree. But instead she said, "It's not your house. It's mine, and Mum's."

And then she walked off and left him there, and asked herself why she felt so miserable.

****

She stayed up late that night watching a film, even though it was boring. It was as if she was scared of going to bed, though she told herself that she was just being stupid. And when she did go, she undressed quickly and got under the covers and left the lamp on, staring up out of the window at the clouds streaming across the moon.

She meant to stay awake. Instead, after what only seemed like seconds, she was being woken.

A small hand was pulling at her, urgent and fierce. With a great rush of fear her eyes opened. She twisted round and his hand clamped over her mouth, his dirty, bony fingers.

"Don't scream," the boy whispered.

Wide-eyed, she nodded.

The boy leaned back on his heels. He took his hand away slowly, and she breathed in the musty smell of him, saw the ear-ring glint in the moon-light.

The lamp was out. All the room was in darkness. Out of the corners of her eyes she thought she saw small curlings of leaves, as if branches were sprouting out of the walls.
A bird fluttered.

"Have you got it?" he asked in an eager voice. He snatched up the box from the table. "Where is it? Where's the key?"

Sarah dragged hair from her face. Her breath came short. She didn't know what to tell him.

Chapter 7
You've Made Me Angry

He must have seen it in her face.

"You didn't get it? I asked you and begged you and you didn't get it!" His narrow face pushed close to hers.

"I tried …" she began, but he reached up and laid his muddy finger across her lips. His eyes were glints of green anger. "Too late," he hissed.

The lamp swayed. As she watched, wide-eyed, it toppled and fell, dragging its flex behind it, breaking the glass shade.

The boy smiled a cold smile. "You've made me angry, Sarah. You've broken your promise. Now I want to break things too."

A breeze was growing in the room, a soft slithering of blown leaves. They flapped along the walls, made the curtains billow. Suddenly all the posters and pictures on her wall began to curl at the corners, rolling up as if they were damp, tugging the Blu-Tak away in long stretchy strings, popping drawing pins out.

She pulled away from him. "Stop it!" she shouted.

He shook his head.

Boxes and bottles crashed on the dressing table. Lids flew off jars of make-up. They rolled and the gloop from them dripped in blobs onto the carpet. Sarah gave a gasp of dismay. All her books fell forward from the bookshelves, one by one, crumpling in an explosion of pages. From the half-opened wardrobe, clothes and scarves began to slither and twist and tear themselves to shreds.

"Stop it! Please!"

"Get me a key," he said.

His fingers caught her arms and held them tight. "Get me a key, Sarah. I won't be trapped here any more. For a hundred years I've wandered this field, before there was a barn, before there was a house. All through the winter nights, through the frost and cold, waiting for someone to hear me, see me, sobbing and crying and scrabbling at the windows." He drew back. "I won't let you go now, Sarah. Not now I've found you."

He was gone so suddenly that she was still staring at the shadow of his outline, and found it was only her coat swinging on the wardrobe door. As she watched, the coat fell in a heap onto the floor.

****

"… never seen such an absolute mess," Mum said crossly. "I should make you stay in and clean every bit of it up."

Sarah chewed toast, only half listening. It was hard to eat. Fear was choking her. And she was so tired. She had over-slept again, and felt heavy and bleary. Mum picked up her coat. "Don't forget. By the time I come back … "

She went out into the hall, still talking. The dogs burst in with a joyful bark. But when the door was opened, they slunk outside and ran towards the gate, ears flat.

Matt came back in.

For a moment they sat in silence. Sarah drank cold tea. Then Matt said, "There's something wrong with the dogs. Can't you tell? It's as if they don't like the house any more. They scratch to go out."

Sarah looked at him blankly.

Then he said, "What's going on, Sarah? Your bedroom looks like it's been hit by a bomb."

"So you looked!"

"Your mother was steaming."

"You shouldn't have gone in." But her answer was flat. She had no energy left to be angry with him. She stood up. "I've got to go into town."

"I'll drive you," he said.

She stared, surprised. "I didn't know you'd passed your test."

Matt gave a shrug. His dark hair flopped in his eyes. "You don't know much about me at all, do you?"

For a moment she felt bad about it. Then she went to get the box.

****

There was a lock-smiths in town and she took the box there. They were very quick. They fiddled and filed and tried various keys until one fitted. As the shop woman turned the key, Sarah heard the lock click and her heart gave a great jump. She put her hand out hard on the box lid so it didn't open.

The woman looked at her oddly. "£6.50, please."

Sarah paid, locked the box again quickly and put it in the plastic bag. But as she walked up past the lane that led to Morgan Rees's shop she stopped. For a moment she wanted to go down there, to talk to him again, to find out what had worried him so much.

The lane was quiet. Leaves lay in puddles. The swans were dabbling in the thick weed that grew on one side of the stream, lifting their long necks and shaking them.

Sarah walked down to the shop and looked in.

41

Morgan Rees had a customer. His back was to her, but he and the customer were talking. She saw Morgan Rees spread a hand out in excitement, then stab a long finger at some paper on the desk.

She put her hand to the door, and then stopped.

The customer had turned around, and she saw it was Matt.

Instantly she ducked back behind a cabinet that filled the window.

They hadn't seen her. But what was Matt doing in an antique shop, Matt with his Goth coat and his black eye-liner? Was he in some sort of plot with Morgan Rees to get the box?

She backed away, knowing now how much she had wanted to go in.

Then the wind gusted in her face, flapped her coat, whipped her hair across her eyes. All the leaves in the puddles lifted and spattered her with mud. Looking up, she saw a small shadow hunched in the dark tunnel at the end of the alley.

"Tonight, Sarah," it whispered.

Chapter 8
Alone

"What do you think?" Sarah's mum turned in front of the mirror.

Sarah said, "Very nice."

"Well, you could be a bit more positive," her mum said with a sigh.

"It's great. It looks really good on you."

Mum's dress was red, and long. Over it she wore a purple and red coat, very off-beat, very arty. Her hair was piled up and bits of it dangled in curls. She looked every bit the famous sculptor.

"I hope so. It'll have to do." She smiled. "I wish you could come, Sarah, I really do, but the invitation was only for two. We'll be back around ten tomorrow morning. Are you sure there isn't someone who you'd like to have to stay for the night? Olly, or Kate?"

"No. Not really."

"I don't like to think of you here on your own."

Sarah gave a shrug. "Matt will be here."

"No, he won't." Mum put her purse and some lipstick in her bag. "He's out late with some friends tonight, Gareth said."

Sarah frowned. Sitting on the window seat, she pulled her knees up and hugged them tight. In the window she watched her own reflection, and beyond it the autumn golds and reds of the landscape. She found herself wishing that Matt were staying home, and that shocked her. Why was she so nervous? She had the key. The boy would be free. It would all be all right.

Downstairs, Gareth was waiting by the fire. He had a blue suit on, and a purple tie that matched Mum's coat.

"Fantastic," he said as she came in.

Mum giggled. "You're not so bad yourself."

They grinned, and Mum arranged his tie. Sarah watched them and almost smiled. Then she realised and gave a scowl. She'd have to watch herself. She was getting soft.

Later, standing at the door and waving goodbye with the dogs panting beside her, she watched the car reverse and vanish up the lane until only its red tail-light showed.

Then that went too. She was alone.

For a moment she listened.

The darkness was damp and windy. She could hear the shed door creaking and branches being stirred, and, far off, the murmur of traffic on the road.

She had never been in the house alone at night before. Suddenly she became aware of how lonely it was. The next neighbours were at the farm three fields away.

Jess nuzzled her hand.

She turned. "All right, girl. I'm coming."

There was no sign of Matt, so she locked up and fed the dogs and ate supper and went to bed.

For a long time she lay awake, waiting, then dozed and woke and dozed again, until in one sudden second she opened her eyes and stared into her pillow.

He was here.

She heard him. Heard a soft slither in the room, smelt that leafy, damp stench. Under the sheets she closed her eyes and breathed a prayer. She was stiff, her body sheened with sweat. Terror hammered under her ribs.

He said, "Sarah."

Slowly she sat up and saw him.

He was sitting on the stool of her dressing table, a shadow in the darkness. One stripe of light from the moon slanted over him, showing her the angle of his jaw, a glint of the copper ring in his ear.

He stood up and came closer. She saw that leaves and clots of mud fell from him. She snapped the lamp switch on. Nothing happened. The room stayed dark.

"Where is it?" he said.

She knelt up among the crumpled bed-clothes. The house was silent. Even the wind seemed to have dropped, and there was no sound from the dogs.

"What have you done to Jack and Jess?"

He shook his head. "They were afraid. The front door opened and they ran out. You'll have to go looking for them in the morning. Where is it, Sarah? Where's my key?"

All she wanted was to end this. She slid her hand under the pillow and felt for it. She found the cold touch of metal and pulled the key out.

His eyes lit with a strange light. He held out his hand for it but she said, "You'll need the box. It's there, on the desk."

With a swift movement he turned, took the silver box and brought it over. His hands stroked it, leaving muddy smears on the perfect oak leaves. He sat on the bed and looked at her. "I've dreamed of this."

"Do ghosts dream?" she whispered.

"All day. While the world turns and people work and talk and forget us, the ghosts dream." He reached out and took the key from her. "And now my dream will come true."

He put the key into the lock and said in a sly voice, "You must turn it for me. I'm a ghost. I can't."

So she turned the key.

Or tried to.

It wouldn't move. She tried again, shook the box, jammed the key in tight.

It wouldn't turn.

The boy snatched it off her. He forced it, struggled with it.

And when he looked up, his pinched face was white and drawn. "You've tricked me!"

"No! I – "

"You've tricked me. You should never have done that, Sarah."

In terror, she grabbed at him. Her fingers closed on cold, empty air. But before she could say anything, she looked past him and saw Matt, standing in the open door of her room, holding up a slim, bright key.

"She didn't trick you," Matt said. "I did."

Chapter 9
A Soul for a Soul

Matt had a torch, but as he came into the room it failed, and the light sparked out. Quickly Sarah jumped up and grabbed the curtains. As she flung them wide a bright flood of moonlight spilled into the room. She saw the boy fixing Matt with a stare of cold hate.

"What have you done?" he hissed.

Matt held the key tight. "Sarah had a key made, but I took it from under her pillow and put another one there. All that one opens is the padlock on my bike."

"You've spoiled everything," the boy snapped.

Sarah shook her head. "But why?"

Matt came in and leaned against the dressing table. "He knows why."

The boy looked down. He clasped his bony hands tight together in silent agony. "I can't tell you," he whispered. "If I do, I'm trapped here for ever."

"Well, you're in luck. Here's someone who can tell her." Matt nudged the door wider with his foot and with a shock Sarah saw that someone else was standing just outside. A tall man in a dark coat, his glasses catching the moonlight. It was Morgan Rees.

He said, "So it's true."

"You!" Sarah was amazed. "How did you ...?"

"He saw me talking to you, and next time I passed there he was waiting for me," Matt said. "He was worried about you."

Morgan Rees was staring intently at the ghost of the boy. "I was very concerned. And now, to see him! I read the words on the box, and I have heard of such spells, but I have never seen – "

"What spells?" Sarah's voice was sharp with anger. "Explain this to me."

Morgan Rees stepped into the moonlight. Rather like Matt, he wore a long, dark coat. For a moment she had the crazy thought that they were like master and apprentice.

"I was dismayed when I read the letters on the box. Let me read them to you now."

"No!" The boy's face was full of anguish. "If you do ... she'll know."

"She has to know." Rees took the box that Sarah held out to him and turned the letters to the light. "This writing is old. The language is Latin. It says that the box is made to hold a soul, and whoever opens the box and frees the soul trapped inside it will, in turn, be punished by having their own soul take its place. This is true, boy, isn't it?"

The boy was still a moment. Then his shoulders sagged. "Yes."

Sarah said, "But you told me ..."

"It was all true, what I told you. Only that the curse was not for all time. It was just until I could get someone to open this, and take my place." His voice was sullen and miserable. "And I nearly did."

She stared at him in horror. "You would have let that happen? To me?"

He gave a shrug and a fragment of mud fell from his shoulders to the floor. "Why should I care who it was? You, him, anyone would do. I'd be free! Free from haunting this darkness, from this terrible cold place! All night I lie in the leaves and the tree sways above me and there's no one!"

She watched him, half angry, half sorry for him. Then she looked at the box, and at Morgan Rees. "What can we do? There has to be something we can do. If it's a spell, surely it can be broken?"

"It's possible," Morgan Rees said, looking at Sarah. "But it will be a risk. Both for you and your brother."

"He's not my brother!"

The tall man frowned. "But I thought …"

"Step-brother." Matt's voice was quiet. "What do you mean, risk? And why us?"

Rees looked grave. "The box is made to hold only one soul. It cannot hold two. If two people open it together, strong in their trust in each other, then the spell would be broken. The curse would shiver into nothingness. Or so I believe ..."

Sarah was dismayed. "You're not sure?"

"Not ... completely sure. But it is all I can suggest."

She felt confused and unhappy. She said, "Yes, but the trouble is that Matt and I ... well, we're not ..."

Her words dried up. She didn't know how to finish. For a moment there was silence, and then she heard the boy sigh. He stood and moved back out of the light, a shadow at the window. He looked out at the moon-lit fields and hills. "I was only a pickpocket. I didn't deserve this. But it's up to you, Sarah."

She was silent a moment. Then she took her dressing gown, wrapped it round herself and tightened the belt. She walked over to Matt and looked right into his face. "I'm sorry. About ... being a bitch. Even though that Goth stuff is stupid."

"I'm sorry you were, too." He grinned. "And I'm sorry about what I said. But do you really want to try this, Sarah? Because if we mess up, one of us might be the ghost that haunts this house for the next hundred years."

She glanced over at the boy, his pale, hopeless face.

"I'm ready if you are."

For a moment Matt was still. Then he turned to Morgan Rees. "All right," he said in a quiet voice. "Tell us what to do."

Chapter 10
Together

In the garden the wind had dropped. The moon lit the smooth lawns, and the air was so cold that Sarah's breath frosted round her face. She was glad of her thick coat and boots.

She looked behind her. The boy stood in the shadows of the house, leaning against the wall, watching. Out here he seemed more frail and helpless than ever. She was sure she could see the bricks of the wall through his body.

Morgan Rees came past her, carrying the box. He walked out to a place on the frosty grass and said, "This will do."

Matt came up behind her. They watched in silence.

The tall man put on his glasses and read the Latin words again, turning the box in the silvery light. He said, "Do you have the key?"

Sarah held it up.

"Then you must unlock it together."

She didn't move.

To her surprise, Matt held out his hand.

"Friends?" he said.

For a moment she hesitated. A sliver of soreness rose in her mind, the pain of memory. Her life as it used to be, just her and Mum, chatting, having fun, being on their own. She had loved it. Then she thought of Mum arranging Gareth's tie, the silly way he had picked purple to match Mum's dress. They were ridiculous. But …

Looking up, she saw Matt watching. She reached out and took his hand, and it was cold and skinny and she felt awkward. "Friends," she muttered. Then, "You idiot."

He grinned. Together they walked towards the box. Morgan Rees held it up so that the moon-light caught it.

The boy flitted closer. He huddled behind Sarah.

She and Matt held the key together. They fitted it into the lock. They turned it, and the click it made was loud in the silent night. Then, together, they lifted the lid of the box.

For a moment she thought it held only darkness.

Then she saw something small and round, faintly shining. As the box tilted it rolled down to one corner. Matt reached in and took it out, and as he held it up they saw to their astonishment that it was nothing more than an acorn.

An acorn shining like silver.

A gasp.

Sarah turned quickly.

The boy cried out. He looked down at himself and they saw that he was fading, that his body was drifting apart like mist on the wind. "I'm going," he breathed. "At last. I'll be there. Soon, I'll be there!"

Sarah couldn't answer. She reached out to touch him but there was nothing left of him, and all at once his shape was a dissolving darkness and a whisper of sound that might have been her name, or might just have been the swish of grasses in the night.

"Goodbye," she whispered. "Sleep tight."

"We did it," Matt said. "And we're still alive."

Sarah nodded. Then, as Morgan Rees took the box from them, she almost dropped it in shock. For, out of the empty box, birds were flying – blue and gold birds with long tails and flashes of scarlet on their wings. They fluttered and sang in an explosion of noise.

Then they flew away, in a great cloud, towards the sunrise.

Matt shook his head and looked into the box. "What else is in this thing?"

Morgan Rees closed it quickly. "Who knows? Perhaps we shouldn't look further. But we have this." He took the acorn from Sarah, held it in his hand for a moment and then gave it back to her. "There's only one thing to do with a seed. And that is to plant it."

She nodded and walked a few steps, choosing the spot carefully. Not too near the house, but out in the lawn, not far from her bedroom. Not far from where the boy's tree had once been, the tree she had seen in the painting, and in her dream.

She bent down and pulled at the grass. It came up in clumps, damp and soggy. Underneath the soil was black.

Matt said, "Use this," and handed her a small twig.

She scooped and prodded and dug with it, and made a deep hole, just big enough. Then she popped the acorn in, covered it over, stamped it down, and stood back.

In silence they gazed down at the grass, almost expecting the tree would grow suddenly and, as if by magic, overnight, like the beanstalk in the story. Matt said, "In a few weeks we'll see it sprout. In a hundred years it will be enormous."

A bird began to sing. Looking up, Sarah saw a streak of dim red light in the east.

Morgan Rees said quietly, "It will be daylight soon. You'd better go inside before your parents get back."

Sarah said, "Thank you for your help. Perhaps you should keep the box."

His hand closed round it and he nodded. "I will keep it safe for you. But I will never sell it."

"I think it's done its job," she said.

Morgan Rees smiled.

Together, she and Matt turned back to the house.